TRANSFORMERS: DEFIANCE
ISSUE NUMBER ONE (OF FOUR)

WRITTEN BY: **CHRIS MOWRY**
BREAKDOWNS BY: **DAN KHANNA**
FINISHES BY: **ANDREW GRIFFITH**
COLORS BY: **JOSH PEREZ**
LETTERS BY: **CHRIS MOWRY**
EDITS BY: **DENTON J. TIPTON**

Somewhere in space exists the planet CYBERTRON. Populated by amazing creatures with the ability to alter their appearances, they exist peacefully. They live to protect an ancient artifact of great power; the ALLSPARK, and to protect it at all costs. Their species has worked with one another to maintain a society built upon learning about their history, while protecting their future. Their fragile civilization is about to be torn apart and their world thrown into chaos as a terrible evil arrives on CYBERTRON, threatening the very lives of those we know as the TRANSFORMERS.

Special thanks to Hasbro's Aaron Archer, Michael Kelly, Amie Lozanski, Val Roca, Ed Lane, Michael Provost, Erin Hillman, Samantha Lomow, and Michael Verrecchia for their invaluable assistance.

To discuss this issue of *Transformers*, join the IDW Insiders, or to check out exclusive Web offers, check out our site:

VISIT US AT
www.abdopublishing.com

Reinforced library bound edition published in 2010 by Spotlight, a division of the ABDO Group, 8000 West 78th Street, Edina, Minnesota 55439. Published by agreement with IDW Publishing. www.idwpublishing.com

Printed in the United States of America, Melrose Park, Illinois.
102009
012010

PRINTED ON RECYCLED PAPER

Library of Congress Cataloging-in-Publication Data

Mowry, Chris.
 Defiance / written by Chris Mowry ; pencils by Dan Khanna, Andrew Griffith, & Don Figueroa
 inks by Andrew Griffith & John Wycough ; colors by Josh Perez ; letters by Chris Mowry.
    v. cm.
 "Transformers, revenge of the fallen, offical movie prequel."
 ISBN 978-1-59961-721-3 (vol. 1) -- ISBN 978-1-59961-722-0 (vol. 2)
 ISBN 978-1-59961-723-7 (vol. 3) -- ISBN 978-1-59961-724-4 (vol. 4)
 1. Graphic novels. I. Transformers, revenge of the fallen (Motion picture) II. Title.
 PZ7.7.M69De 2010
 741.5'973--dc22
                            2009036394

All Spotlight books have reinforced library bindings and
are manufactured in the United States of America.

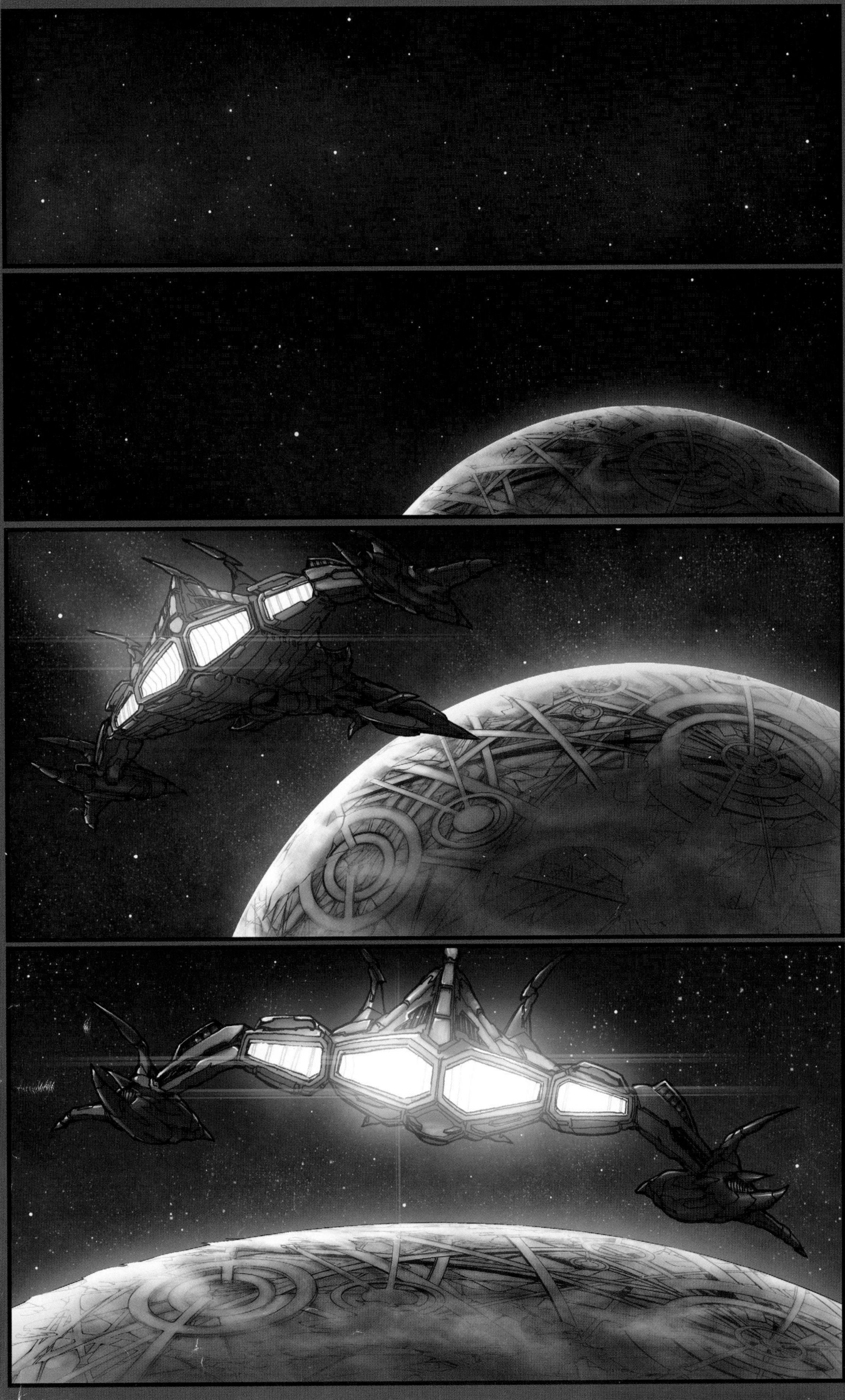

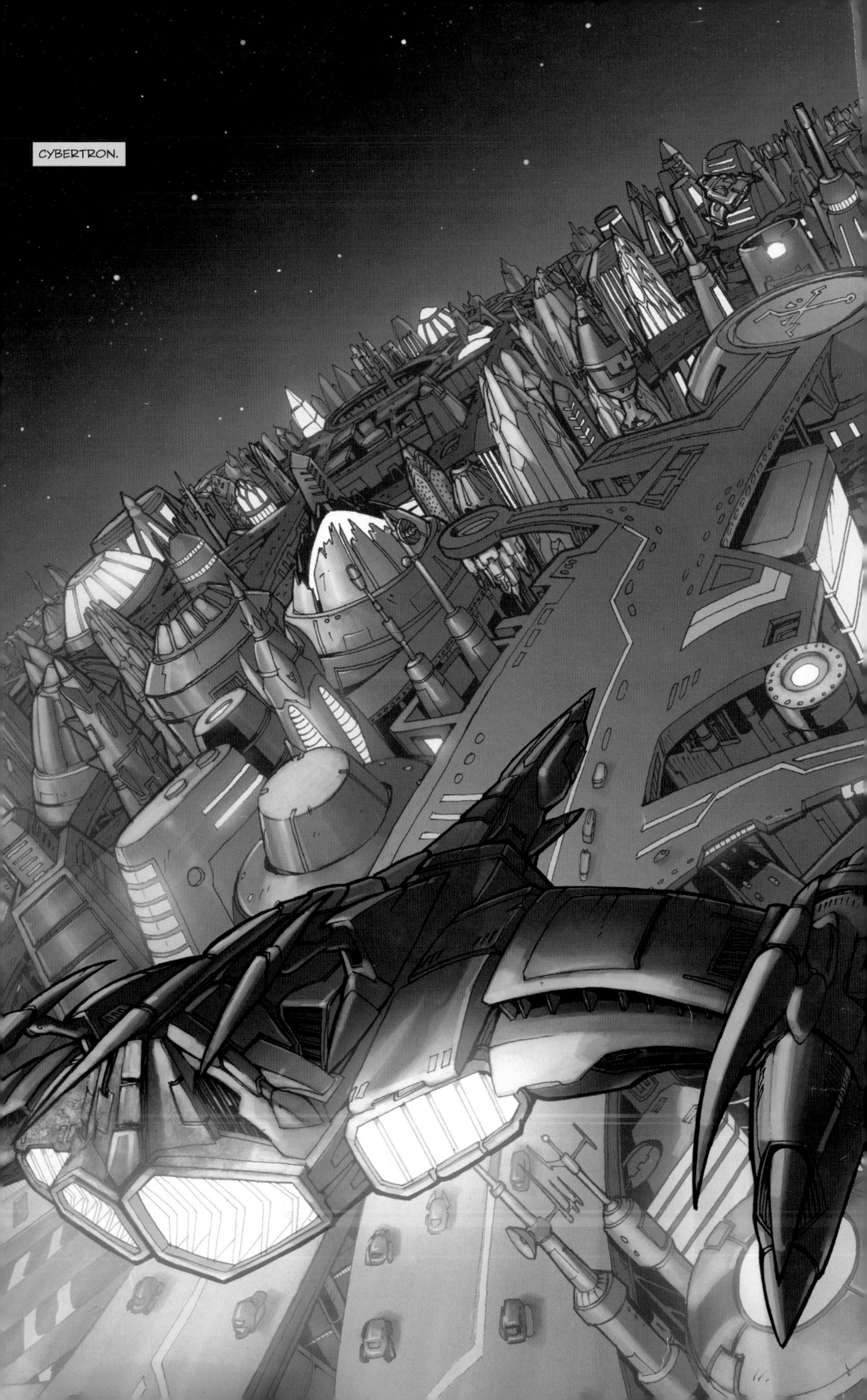
CYBERTRON.

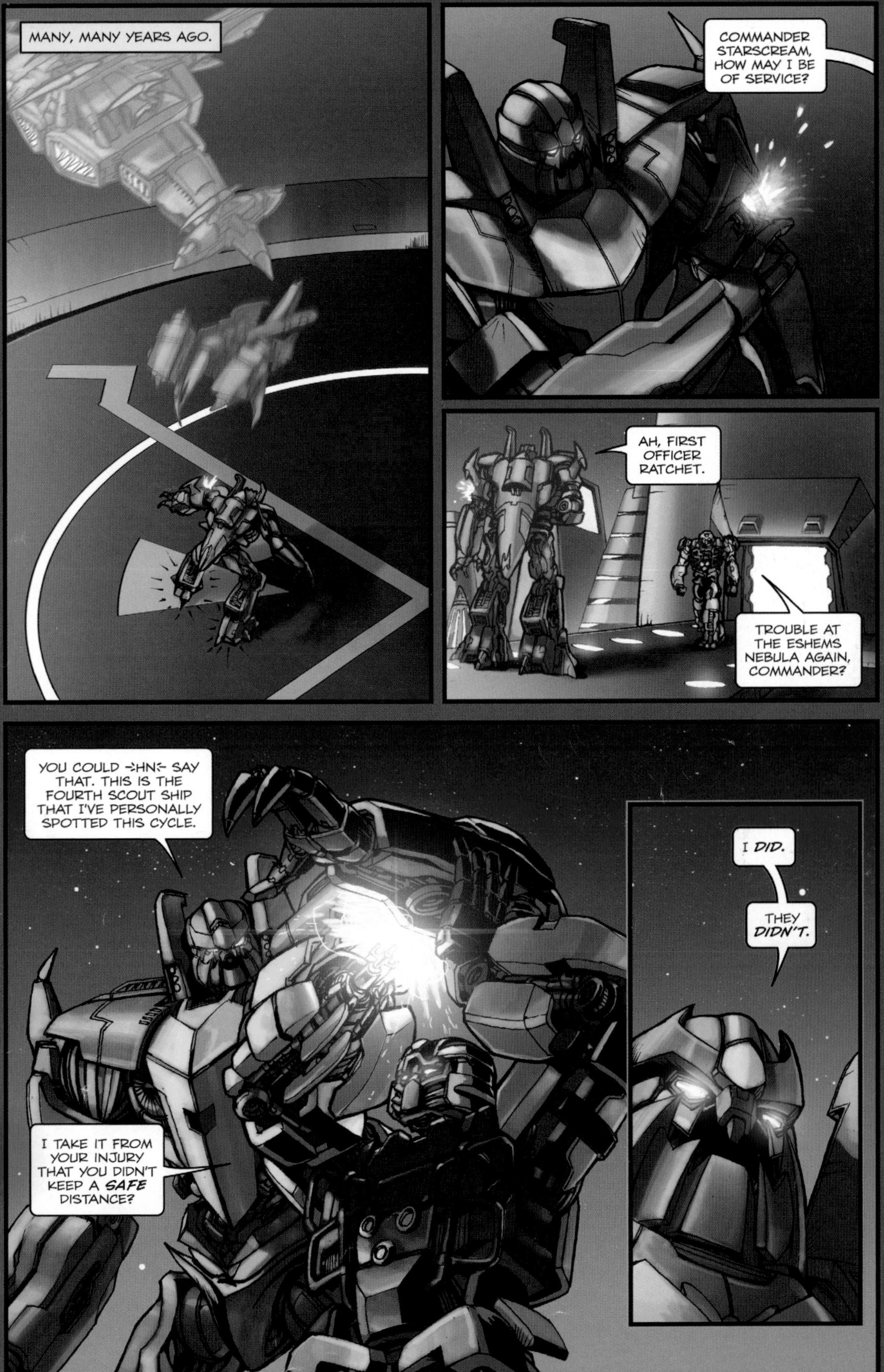
MANY, MANY YEARS AGO.
COMMANDER STARSCREAM, HOW MAY I BE OF SERVICE?
AH, FIRST OFFICER RATCHET.
TROUBLE AT THE ESHEMS NEBULA AGAIN, COMMANDER?
YOU COULD -HN- SAY THAT. THIS IS THE FOURTH SCOUT SHIP THAT I'VE PERSONALLY SPOTTED THIS CYCLE.
I TAKE IT FROM YOUR INJURY THAT YOU DIDN'T KEEP A SAFE DISTANCE?
I DID.
THEY DIDN'T.

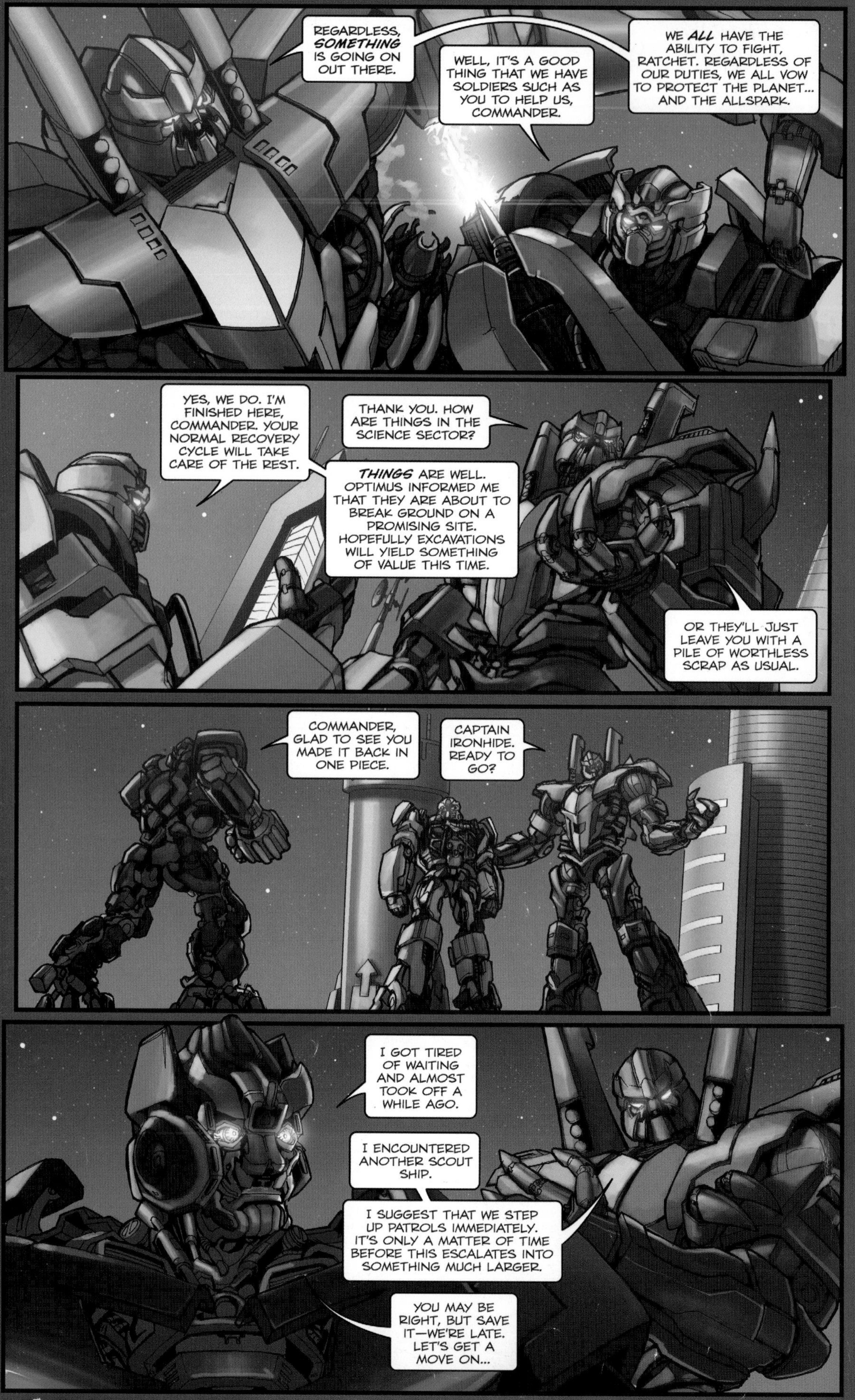
REGARDLESS, SOMETHING IS GOING ON OUT THERE.
WELL, IT'S A GOOD THING THAT WE HAVE SOLDIERS SUCH AS YOU TO HELP US, COMMANDER.
WE ALL HAVE THE ABILITY TO FIGHT, RATCHET. REGARDLESS OF OUR DUTIES, WE ALL VOW TO PROTECT THE PLANET... AND THE ALLSPARK.
YES, WE DO. I'M FINISHED HERE, COMMANDER. YOUR NORMAL RECOVERY CYCLE WILL TAKE CARE OF THE REST.
THANK YOU. HOW ARE THINGS IN THE SCIENCE SECTOR?
THINGS ARE WELL. OPTIMUS INFORMED ME THAT THEY ARE ABOUT TO BREAK GROUND ON A PROMISING SITE. HOPEFULLY EXCAVATIONS WILL YIELD SOMETHING OF VALUE THIS TIME.
OR THEY'LL JUST LEAVE YOU WITH A PILE OF WORTHLESS SCRAP AS USUAL.
COMMANDER, GLAD TO SEE YOU MADE IT BACK IN ONE PIECE.
CAPTAIN IRONHIDE. READY TO GO?
I GOT TIRED OF WAITING AND ALMOST TOOK OFF A WHILE AGO.
I ENCOUNTERED ANOTHER SCOUT SHIP.
I SUGGEST THAT WE STEP UP PATROLS IMMEDIATELY. IT'S ONLY A MATTER OF TIME BEFORE THIS ESCALATES INTO SOMETHING MUCH LARGER.
YOU MAY BE RIGHT, BUT SAVE IT—WE'RE LATE. LET'S GET A MOVE ON...

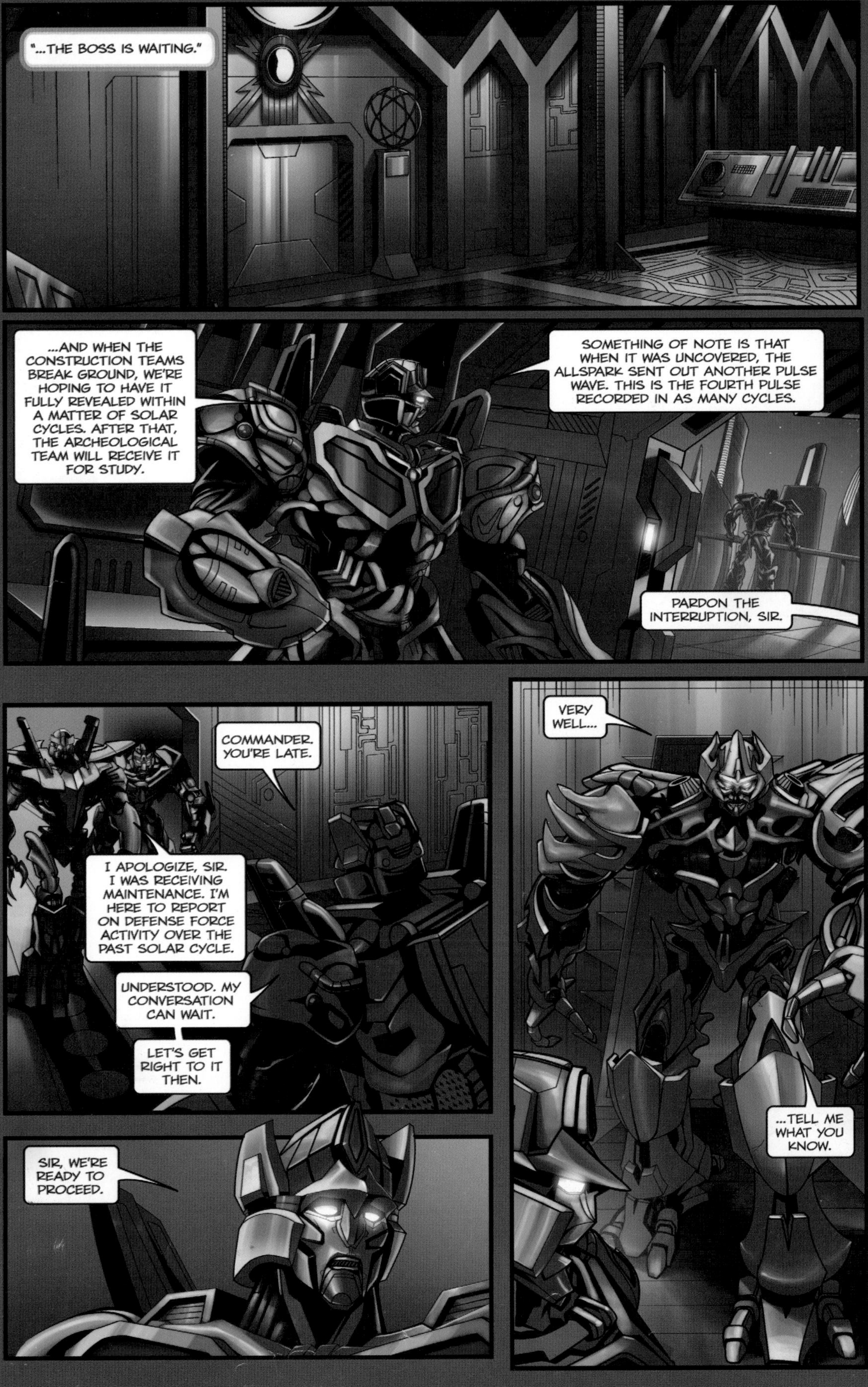
"...THE BOSS IS WAITING."
...AND WHEN THE CONSTRUCTION TEAMS BREAK GROUND, WE'RE HOPING TO HAVE IT FULLY REVEALED WITHIN A MATTER OF SOLAR CYCLES. AFTER THAT, THE ARCHEOLOGICAL TEAM WILL RECEIVE IT FOR STUDY.
SOMETHING OF NOTE IS THAT WHEN IT WAS UNCOVERED, THE ALLSPARK SENT OUT ANOTHER PULSE WAVE. THIS IS THE FOURTH PULSE RECORDED IN AS MANY CYCLES.
PARDON THE INTERRUPTION, SIR.
COMMANDER. YOU'RE LATE.
I APOLOGIZE, SIR. I WAS RECEIVING MAINTENANCE. I'M HERE TO REPORT ON DEFENSE FORCE ACTIVITY OVER THE PAST SOLAR CYCLE.
UNDERSTOOD. MY CONVERSATION CAN WAIT.
LET'S GET RIGHT TO IT THEN.
SIR, WE'RE READY TO PROCEED.
VERY WELL...
...TELL ME WHAT YOU KNOW.

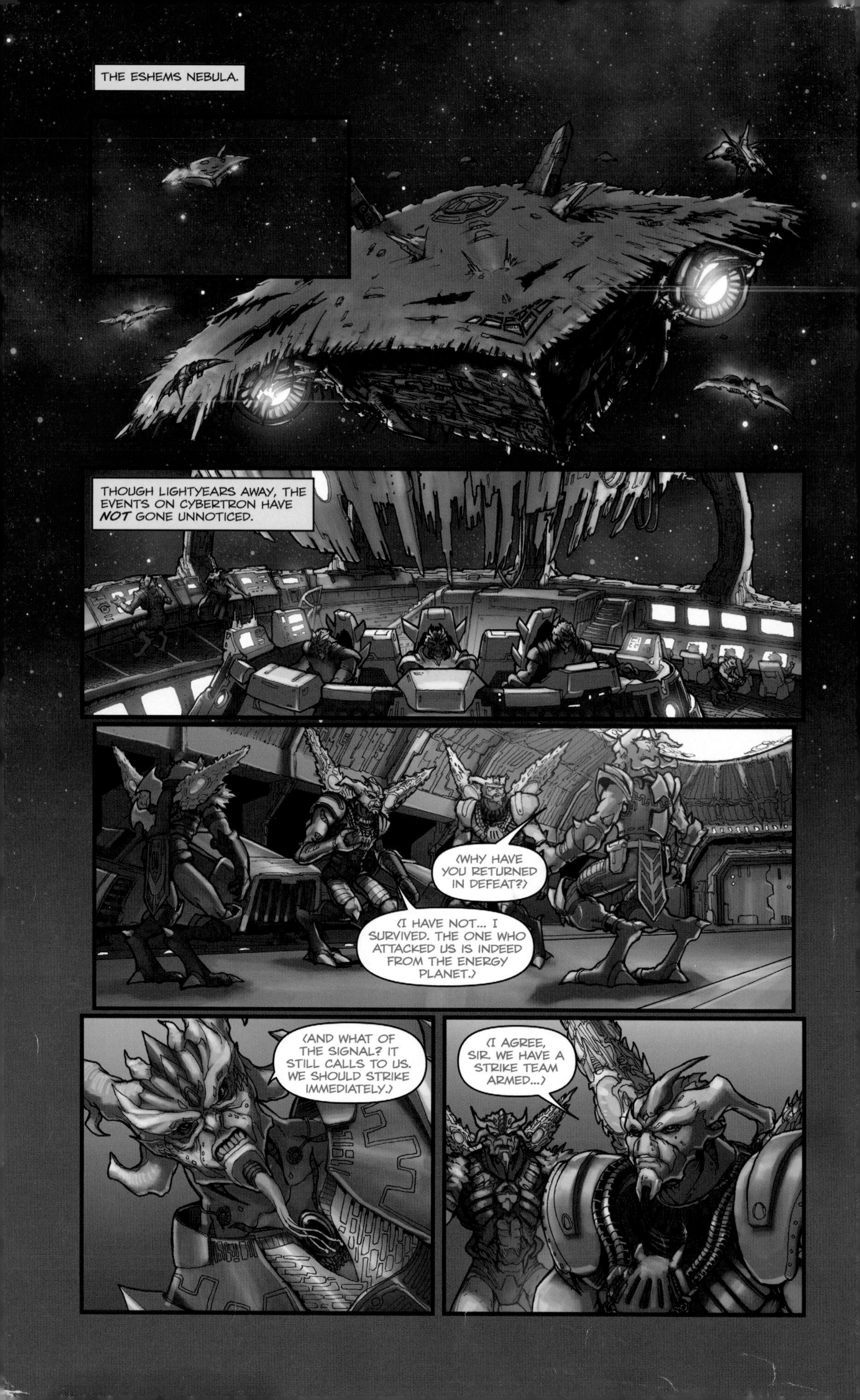

THE ESHEMS NEBULA.
THOUGH LIGHTYEARS AWAY, THE EVENTS ON CYBERTRON HAVE *NOT* GONE UNNOTICED.
(WHY HAVE YOU RETURNED IN DEFEAT?)
(I HAVE NOT... I SURVIVED. THE ONE WHO ATTACKED US IS INDEED FROM THE ENERGY PLANET.)
(AND WHAT OF THE SIGNAL? IT STILL CALLS TO US. WE SHOULD STRIKE IMMEDIATELY.)
(I AGREE, SIR. WE HAVE A STRIKE TEAM ARMED...)

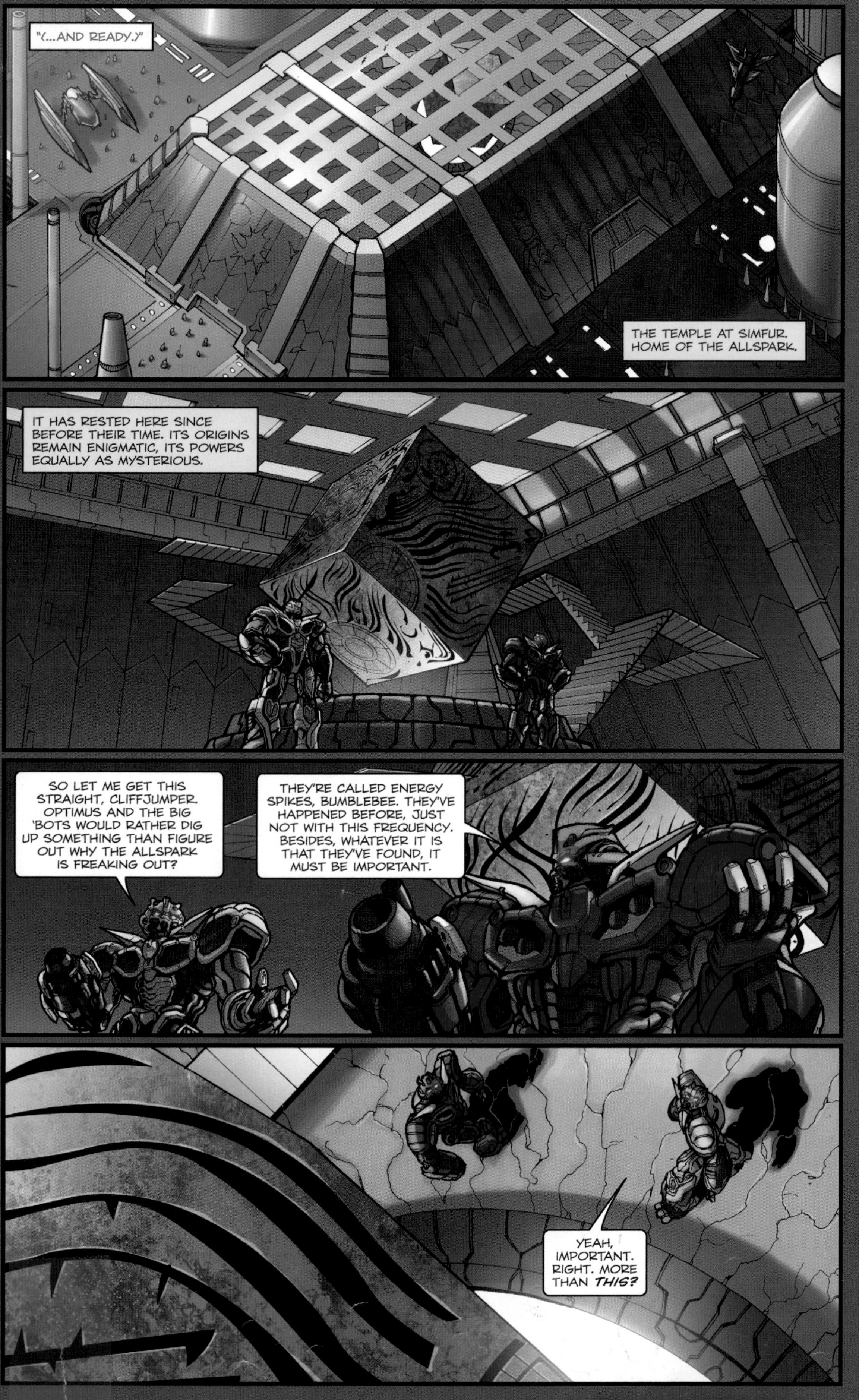
"(...AND READY.)"
THE TEMPLE AT SIMFUR. HOME OF THE ALLSPARK.
IT HAS RESTED HERE SINCE BEFORE THEIR TIME. ITS ORIGINS REMAIN ENIGMATIC, ITS POWERS EQUALLY AS MYSTERIOUS.
SO LET ME GET THIS STRAIGHT, CLIFFJUMPER. OPTIMUS AND THE BIG 'BOTS WOULD RATHER DIG UP SOMETHING THAN FIGURE OUT WHY THE ALLSPARK IS FREAKING OUT?
THEY'RE CALLED ENERGY SPIKES, BUMBLEBEE. THEY'VE HAPPENED BEFORE, JUST NOT WITH THIS FREQUENCY. BESIDES, WHATEVER IT IS THAT THEY'VE FOUND, IT MUST BE IMPORTANT.
YEAH, IMPORTANT. RIGHT. MORE THAN *THIS?*

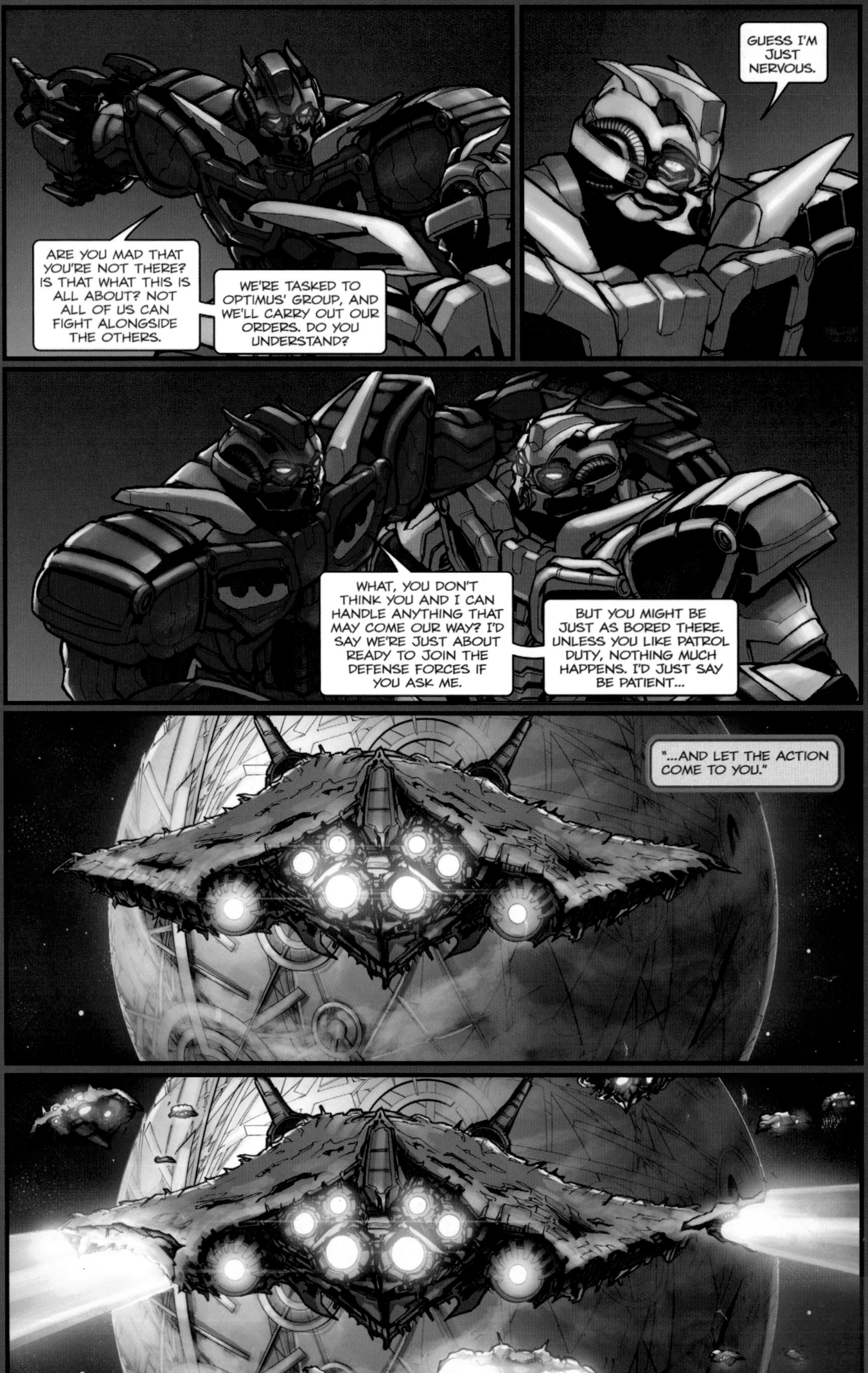
ARE YOU MAD THAT YOU'RE NOT THERE? IS THAT WHAT THIS IS ALL ABOUT? NOT ALL OF US CAN FIGHT ALONGSIDE THE OTHERS.
WE'RE TASKED TO OPTIMUS' GROUP, AND WE'LL CARRY OUT OUR ORDERS. DO YOU UNDERSTAND?
GUESS I'M JUST NERVOUS.
WHAT, YOU DON'T THINK YOU AND I CAN HANDLE ANYTHING THAT MAY COME OUR WAY? I'D SAY WE'RE JUST ABOUT READY TO JOIN THE DEFENSE FORCES IF YOU ASK ME.
BUT YOU MIGHT BE JUST AS BORED THERE. UNLESS YOU LIKE PATROL DUTY, NOTHING MUCH HAPPENS. I'D JUST SAY BE PATIENT...
"...AND LET THE ACTION COME TO YOU."

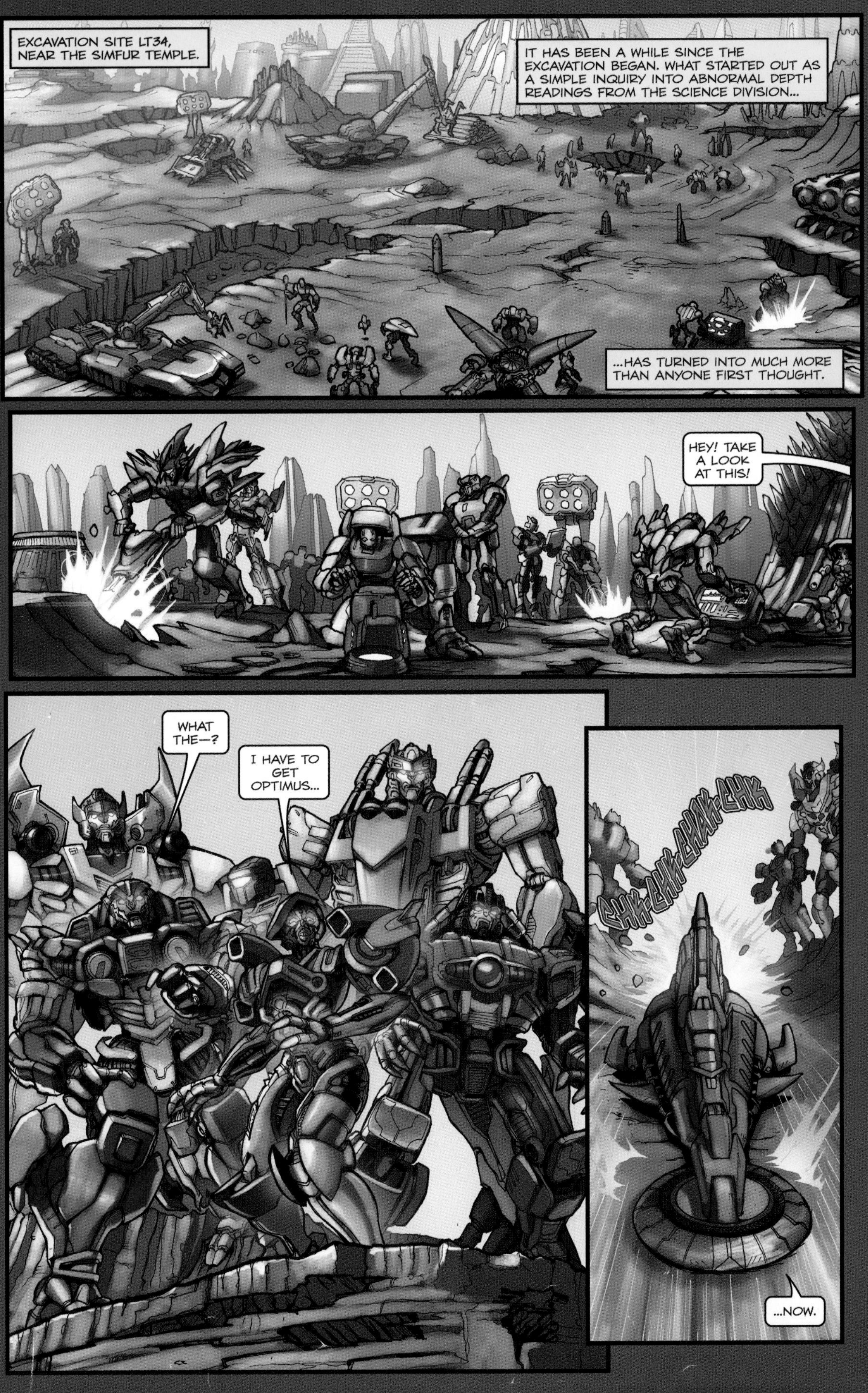
EXCAVATION SITE LT34, NEAR THE SIMFUR TEMPLE.
IT HAS BEEN A WHILE SINCE THE EXCAVATION BEGAN. WHAT STARTED OUT AS A SIMPLE INQUIRY INTO ABNORMAL DEPTH READINGS FROM THE SCIENCE DIVISION...
...HAS TURNED INTO MUCH MORE THAN ANYONE FIRST THOUGHT.
HEY! TAKE A LOOK AT THIS!
WHAT THE—?
I HAVE TO GET OPTIMUS...
CHK-CHK-CHAK-CHK
...NOW.

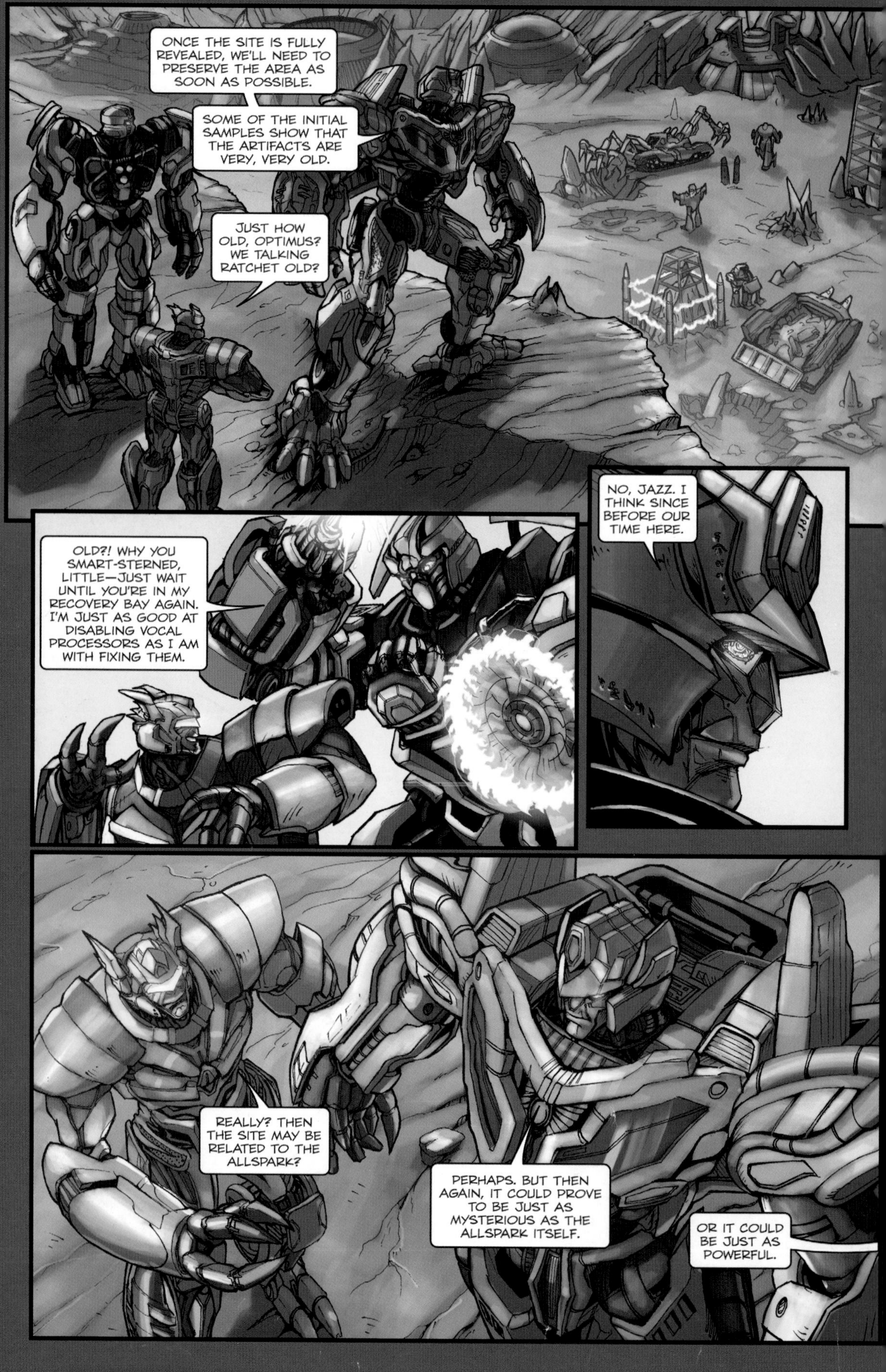

ONCE THE SITE IS FULLY REVEALED, WE'LL NEED TO PRESERVE THE AREA AS SOON AS POSSIBLE.
SOME OF THE INITIAL SAMPLES SHOW THAT THE ARTIFACTS ARE VERY, VERY OLD.
JUST HOW OLD, OPTIMUS? WE TALKING RATCHET OLD?
OLD?! WHY YOU SMART-STERNED, LITTLE—JUST WAIT UNTIL YOU'RE IN MY RECOVERY BAY AGAIN. I'M JUST AS GOOD AT DISABLING VOCAL PROCESSORS AS I AM WITH FIXING THEM.
NO, JAZZ. I THINK SINCE BEFORE OUR TIME HERE.
REALLY? THEN THE SITE MAY BE RELATED TO THE ALLSPARK?
PERHAPS. BUT THEN AGAIN, IT COULD PROVE TO BE JUST AS MYSTERIOUS AS THE ALLSPARK ITSELF.
OR IT COULD BE JUST AS POWERFUL.

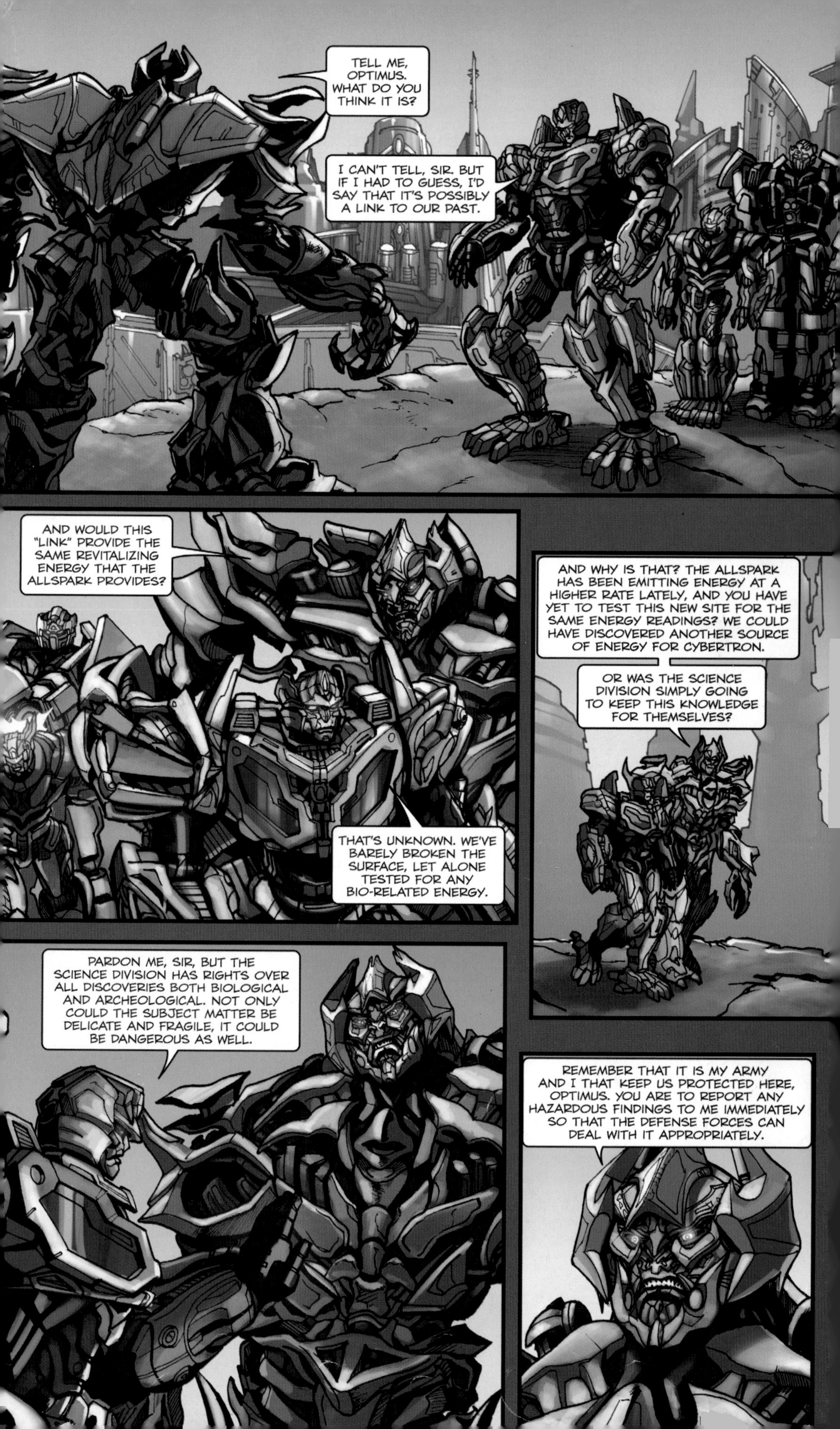
TELL ME, OPTIMUS. WHAT DO YOU THINK IT IS?
I CAN'T TELL, SIR. BUT IF I HAD TO GUESS, I'D SAY THAT IT'S POSSIBLY A LINK TO OUR PAST.
AND WOULD THIS "LINK" PROVIDE THE SAME REVITALIZING ENERGY THAT THE ALLSPARK PROVIDES?
THAT'S UNKNOWN. WE'VE BARELY BROKEN THE SURFACE, LET ALONE TESTED FOR ANY BIO-RELATED ENERGY.
AND WHY IS THAT? THE ALLSPARK HAS BEEN EMITTING ENERGY AT A HIGHER RATE LATELY, AND YOU HAVE YET TO TEST THIS NEW SITE FOR THE SAME ENERGY READINGS? WE COULD HAVE DISCOVERED ANOTHER SOURCE OF ENERGY FOR CYBERTRON.
OR WAS THE SCIENCE DIVISION SIMPLY GOING TO KEEP THIS KNOWLEDGE FOR THEMSELVES?
PARDON ME, SIR, BUT THE SCIENCE DIVISION HAS RIGHTS OVER ALL DISCOVERIES BOTH BIOLOGICAL AND ARCHEOLOGICAL. NOT ONLY COULD THE SUBJECT MATTER BE DELICATE AND FRAGILE, IT COULD BE DANGEROUS AS WELL.
REMEMBER THAT IT IS MY ARMY AND I THAT KEEP US PROTECTED HERE, OPTIMUS. YOU ARE TO REPORT ANY HAZARDOUS FINDINGS TO ME IMMEDIATELY SO THAT THE DEFENSE FORCES CAN DEAL WITH IT APPROPRIATELY.

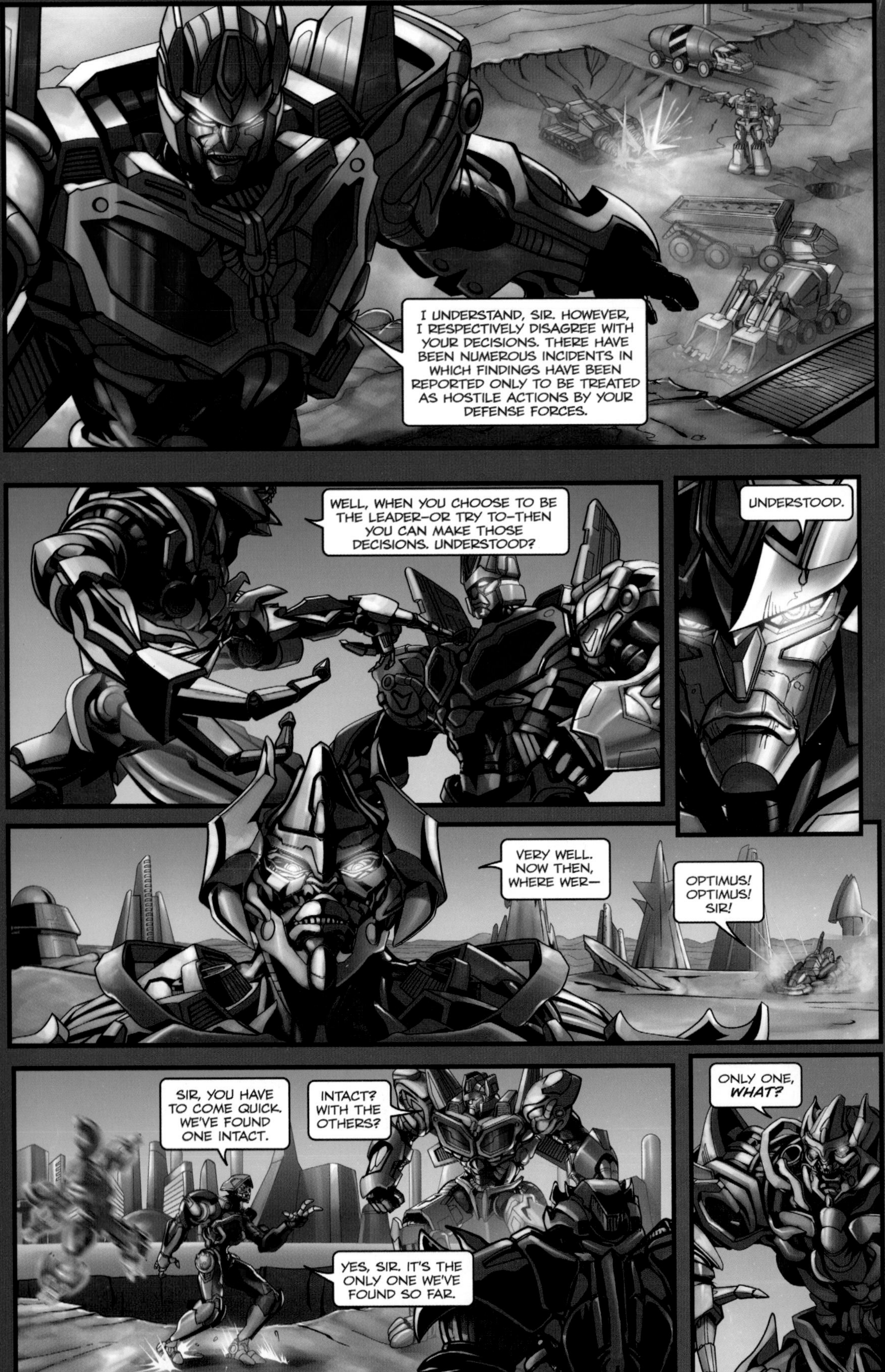
I UNDERSTAND, SIR. HOWEVER, I RESPECTIVELY DISAGREE WITH YOUR DECISIONS. THERE HAVE BEEN NUMEROUS INCIDENTS IN WHICH FINDINGS HAVE BEEN REPORTED ONLY TO BE TREATED AS HOSTILE ACTIONS BY YOUR DEFENSE FORCES.
WELL, WHEN YOU CHOOSE TO BE THE LEADER—OR TRY TO—THEN YOU CAN MAKE THOSE DECISIONS. UNDERSTOOD?
UNDERSTOOD.
VERY WELL. NOW THEN, WHERE WER—
OPTIMUS! OPTIMUS! SIR!
SIR, YOU HAVE TO COME QUICK. WE'VE FOUND ONE INTACT.
INTACT? WITH THE OTHERS?
YES, SIR. IT'S THE ONLY ONE WE'VE FOUND SO FAR.
ONLY ONE, *WHAT?*

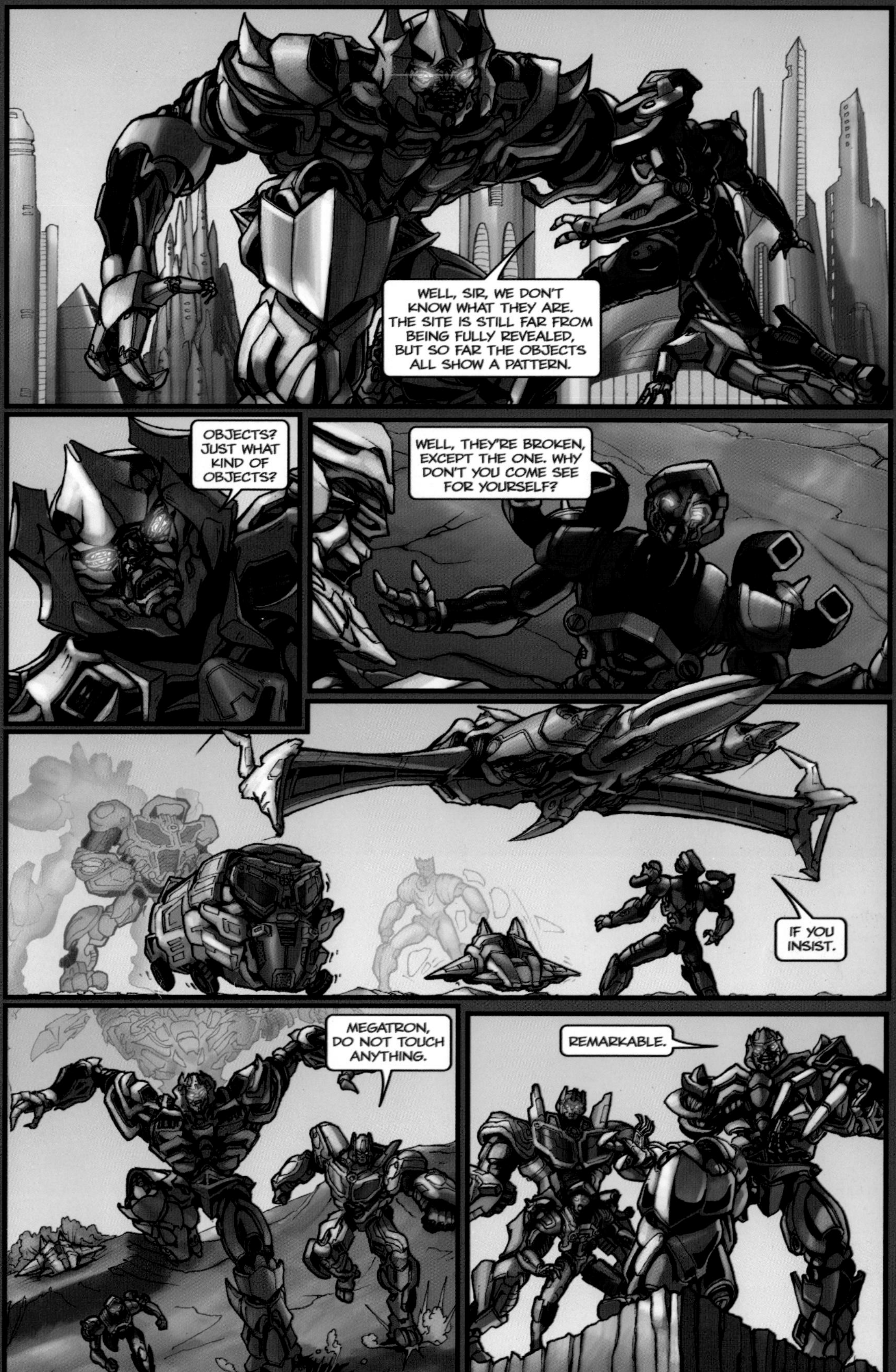
WELL, SIR, WE DON'T KNOW WHAT THEY ARE. THE SITE IS STILL FAR FROM BEING FULLY REVEALED, BUT SO FAR THE OBJECTS ALL SHOW A PATTERN.
OBJECTS? JUST WHAT KIND OF OBJECTS?
WELL, THEY'RE BROKEN, EXCEPT THE ONE. WHY DON'T YOU COME SEE FOR YOURSELF?
IF YOU INSIST.
MEGATRON, DO NOT TOUCH ANYTHING.
REMARKABLE.

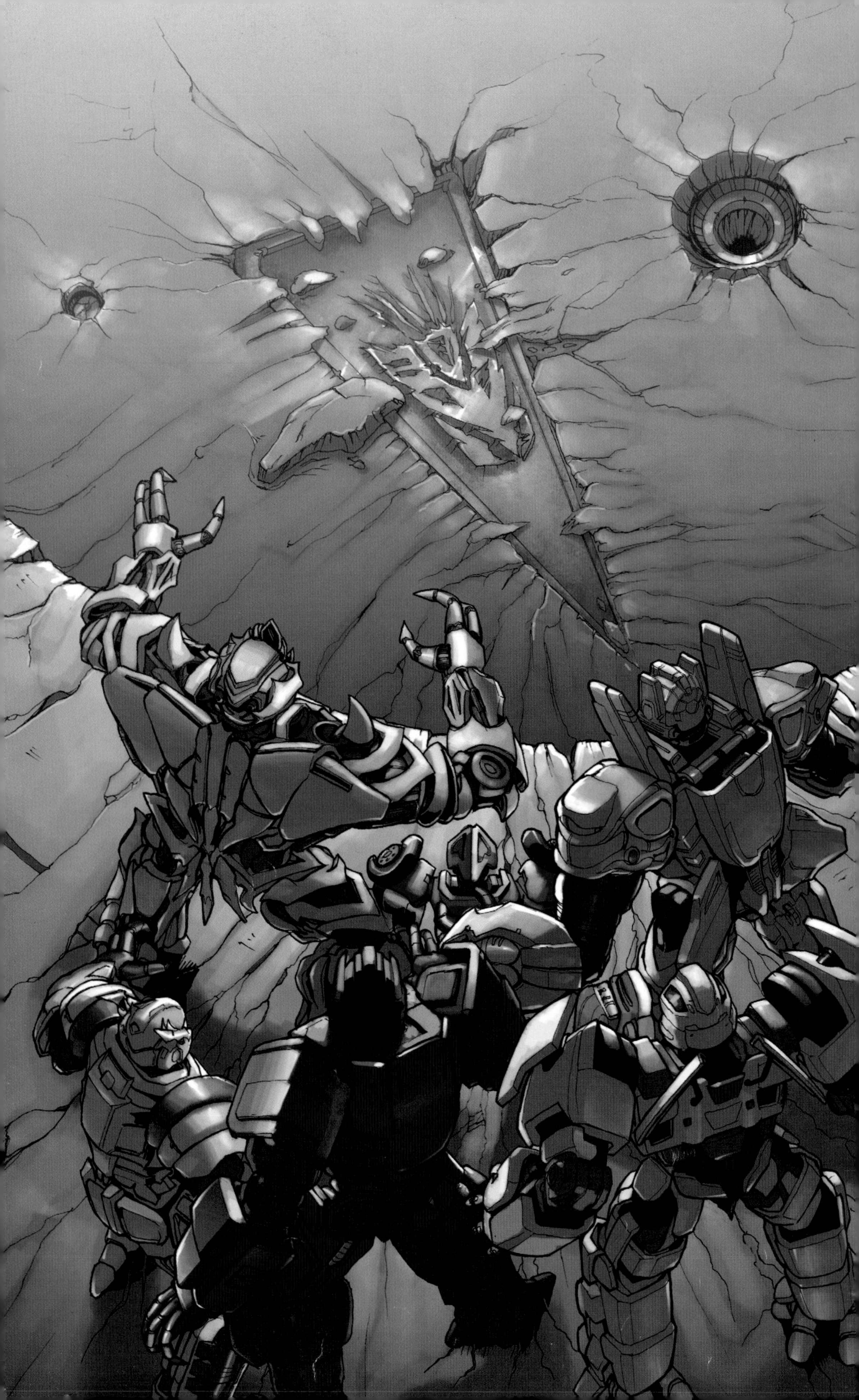

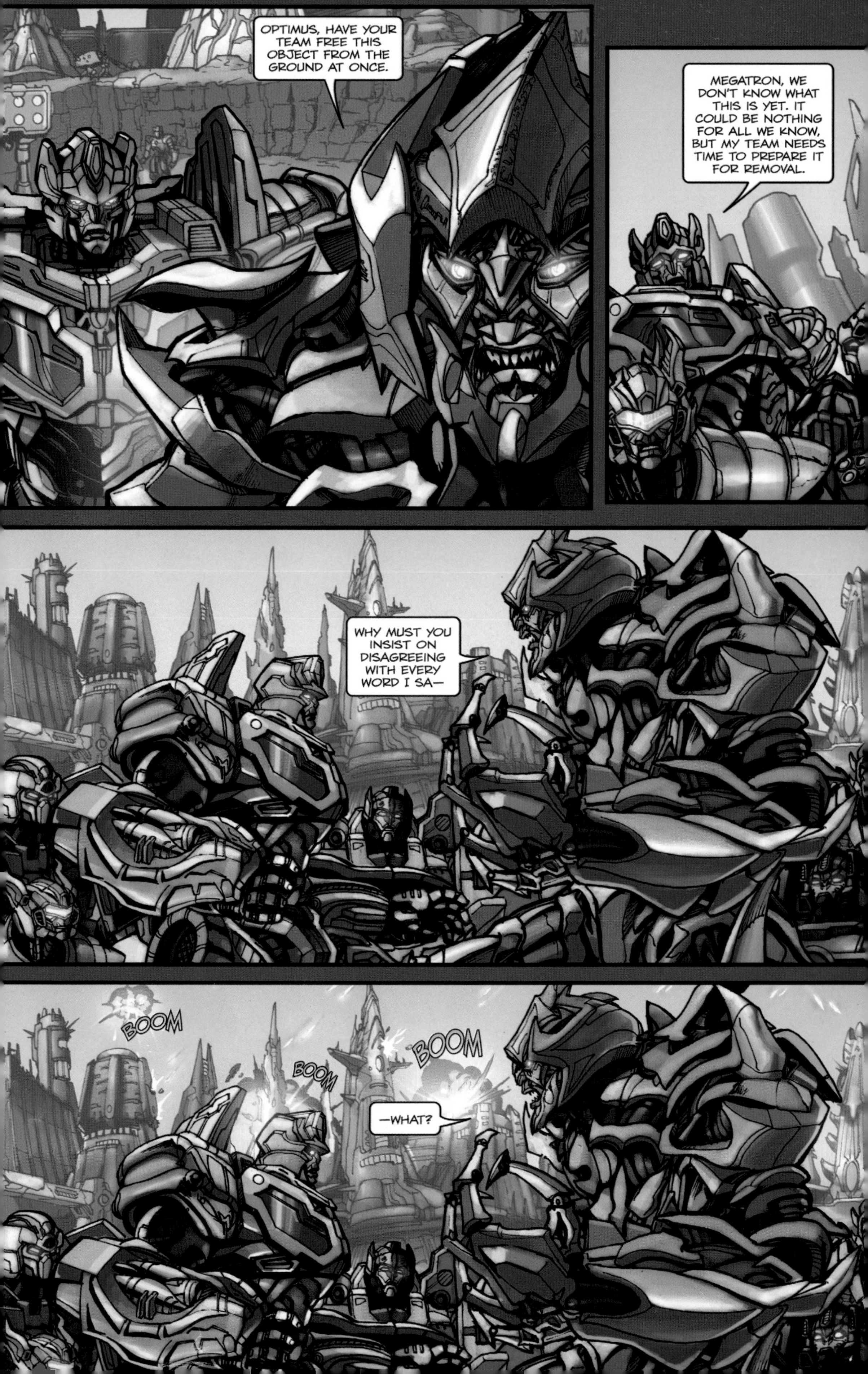
OPTIMUS, HAVE YOUR TEAM FREE THIS OBJECT FROM THE GROUND AT ONCE.
MEGATRON, WE DON'T KNOW WHAT THIS IS YET. IT COULD BE NOTHING FOR ALL WE KNOW, BUT MY TEAM NEEDS TIME TO PREPARE IT FOR REMOVAL.
WHY MUST YOU INSIST ON DISAGREEING WITH EVERY WORD I SA—
BOOM
BOOM
BOOM
—WHAT?

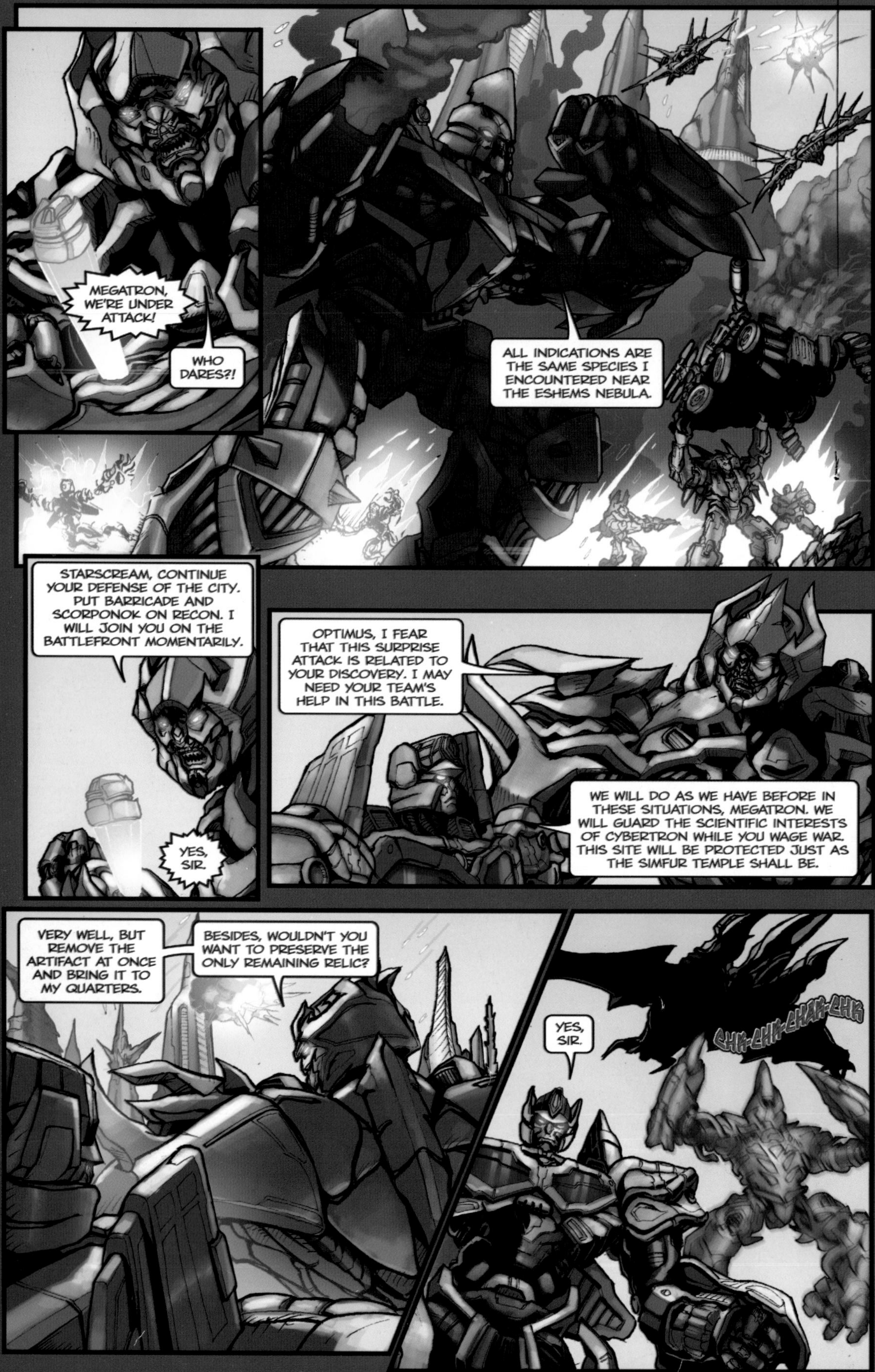
MEGATRON, WE'RE UNDER ATTACK!
WHO DARES?!
ALL INDICATIONS ARE THE SAME SPECIES I ENCOUNTERED NEAR THE ESHEMS NEBULA.
STARSCREAM, CONTINUE YOUR DEFENSE OF THE CITY. PUT BARRICADE AND SCORPONOK ON RECON. I WILL JOIN YOU ON THE BATTLEFRONT MOMENTARILY.
YES, SIR.
OPTIMUS, I FEAR THAT THIS SURPRISE ATTACK IS RELATED TO YOUR DISCOVERY. I MAY NEED YOUR TEAM'S HELP IN THIS BATTLE.
WE WILL DO AS WE HAVE BEFORE IN THESE SITUATIONS, MEGATRON. WE WILL GUARD THE SCIENTIFIC INTERESTS OF CYBERTRON WHILE YOU WAGE WAR. THIS SITE WILL BE PROTECTED JUST AS THE SIMFUR TEMPLE SHALL BE.
VERY WELL, BUT REMOVE THE ARTIFACT AT ONCE AND BRING IT TO MY QUARTERS.
BESIDES, WOULDN'T YOU WANT TO PRESERVE THE ONLY REMAINING RELIC?
YES, SIR.
CHK-CHK-CHAK-CHK

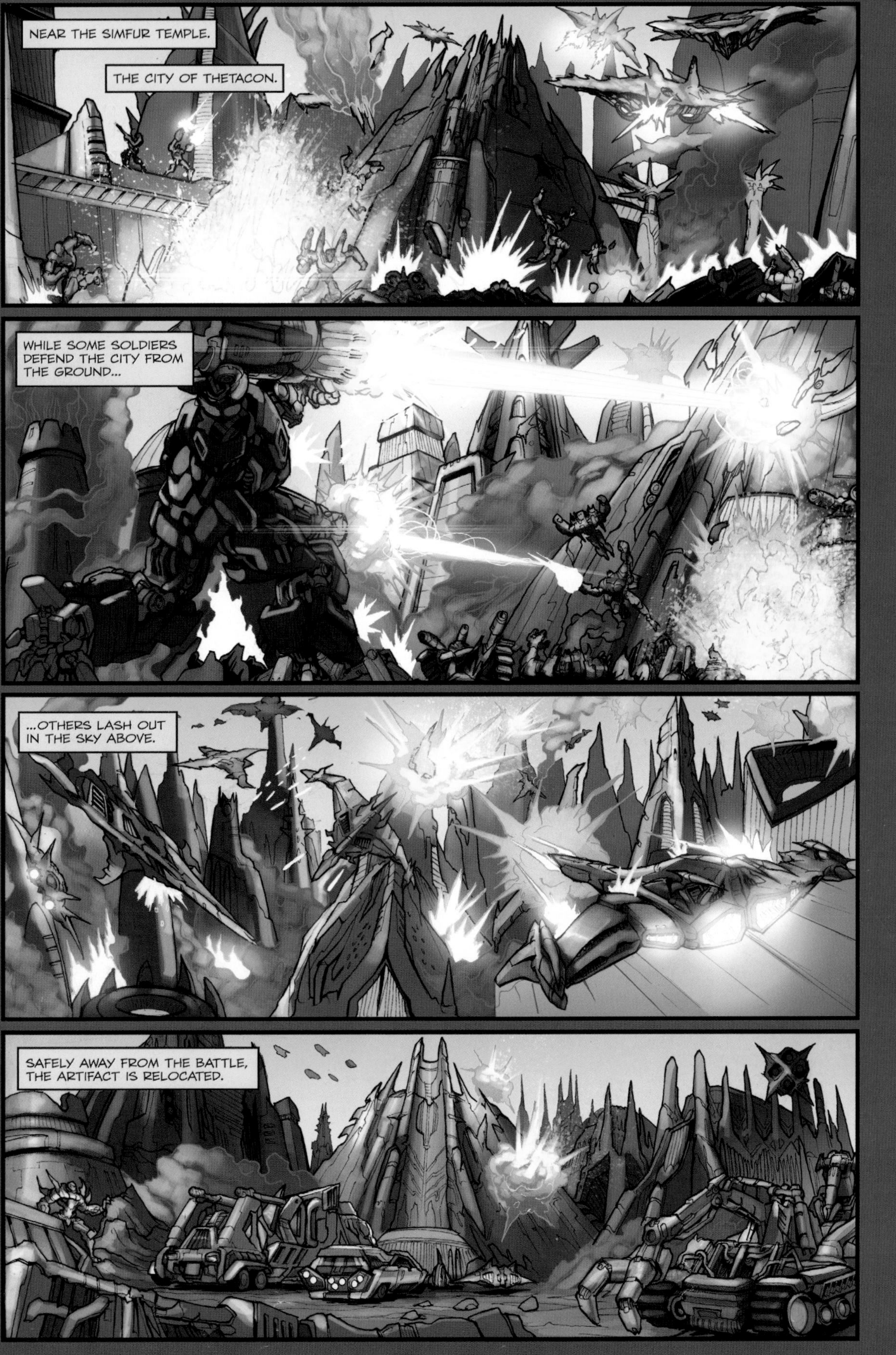
NEAR THE SIMFUR TEMPLE.
THE CITY OF THETACON.
WHILE SOME SOLDIERS DEFEND THE CITY FROM THE GROUND...
...OTHERS LASH OUT IN THE SKY ABOVE.
SAFELY AWAY FROM THE BATTLE, THE ARTIFACT IS RELOCATED.

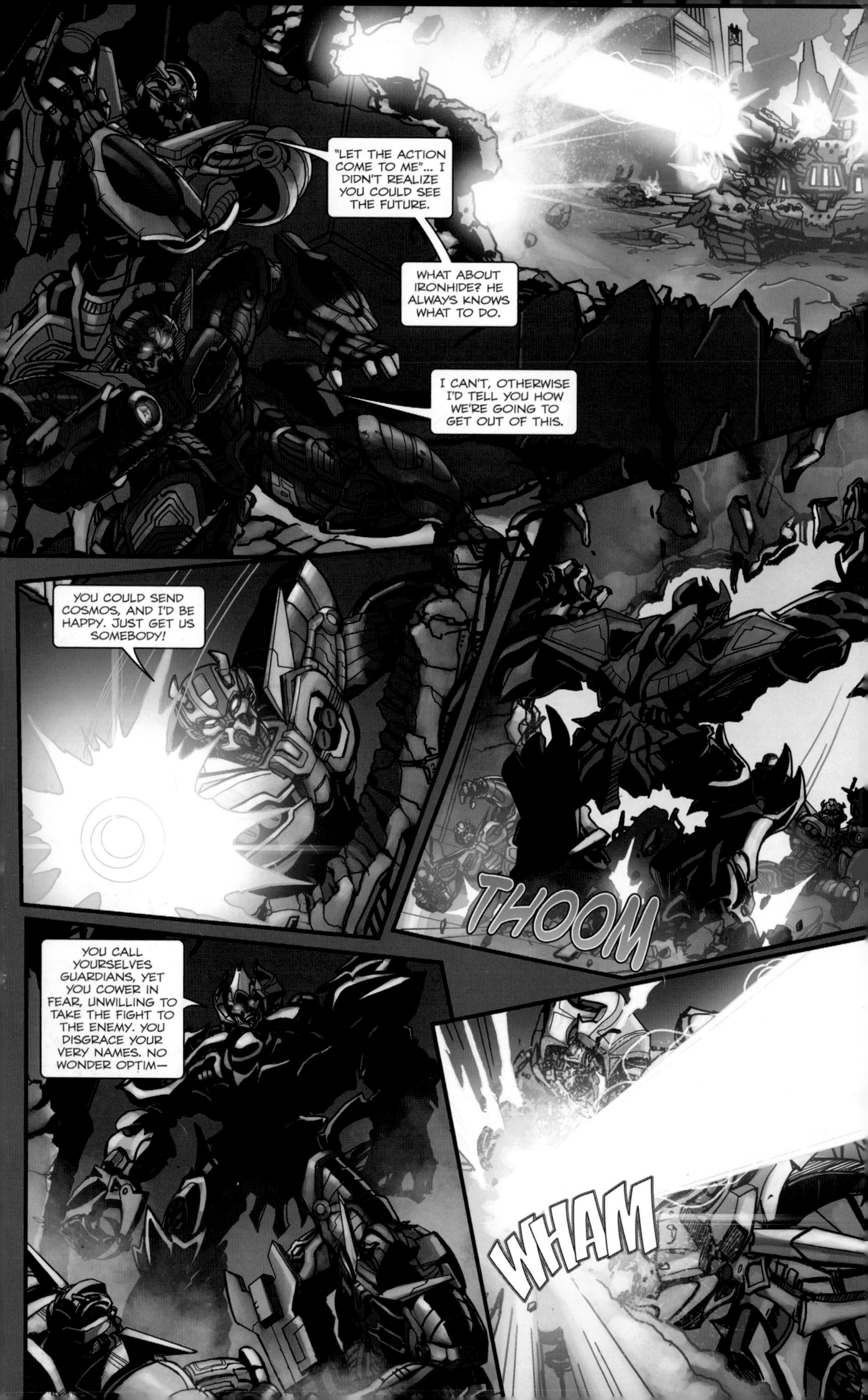
"LET THE ACTION COME TO ME"... I DIDN'T REALIZE YOU COULD SEE THE FUTURE.
WHAT ABOUT IRONHIDE? HE ALWAYS KNOWS WHAT TO DO.
I CAN'T, OTHERWISE I'D TELL YOU HOW WE'RE GOING TO GET OUT OF THIS.
YOU COULD SEND COSMOS, AND I'D BE HAPPY. JUST GET US SOMEBODY!
THOOM
YOU CALL YOURSELVES GUARDIANS, YET YOU COWER IN FEAR, UNWILLING TO TAKE THE FIGHT TO THE ENEMY. YOU DISGRACE YOUR VERY NAMES. NO WONDER OPTIM—
WHAM

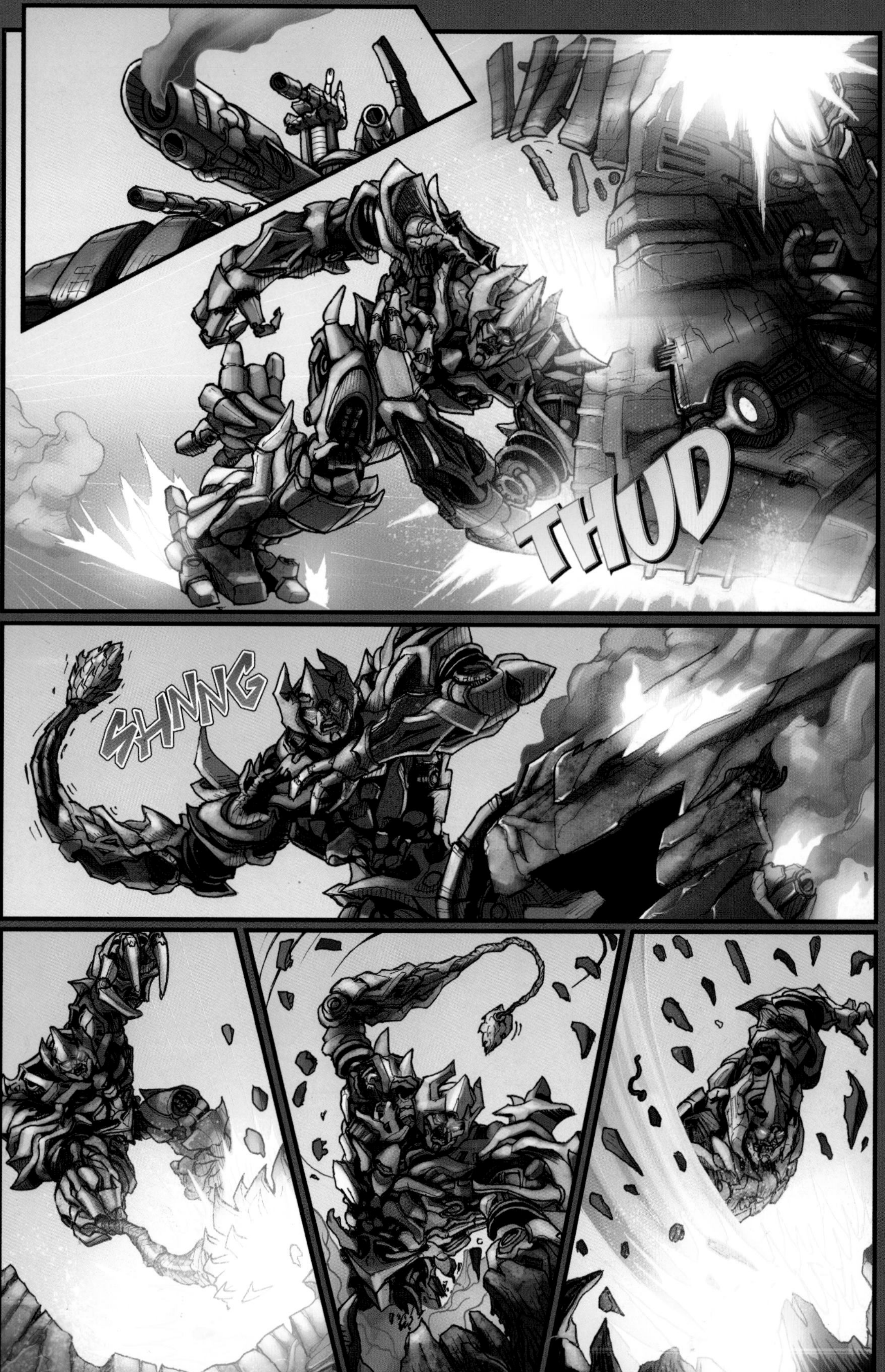
THUD
SHNNG

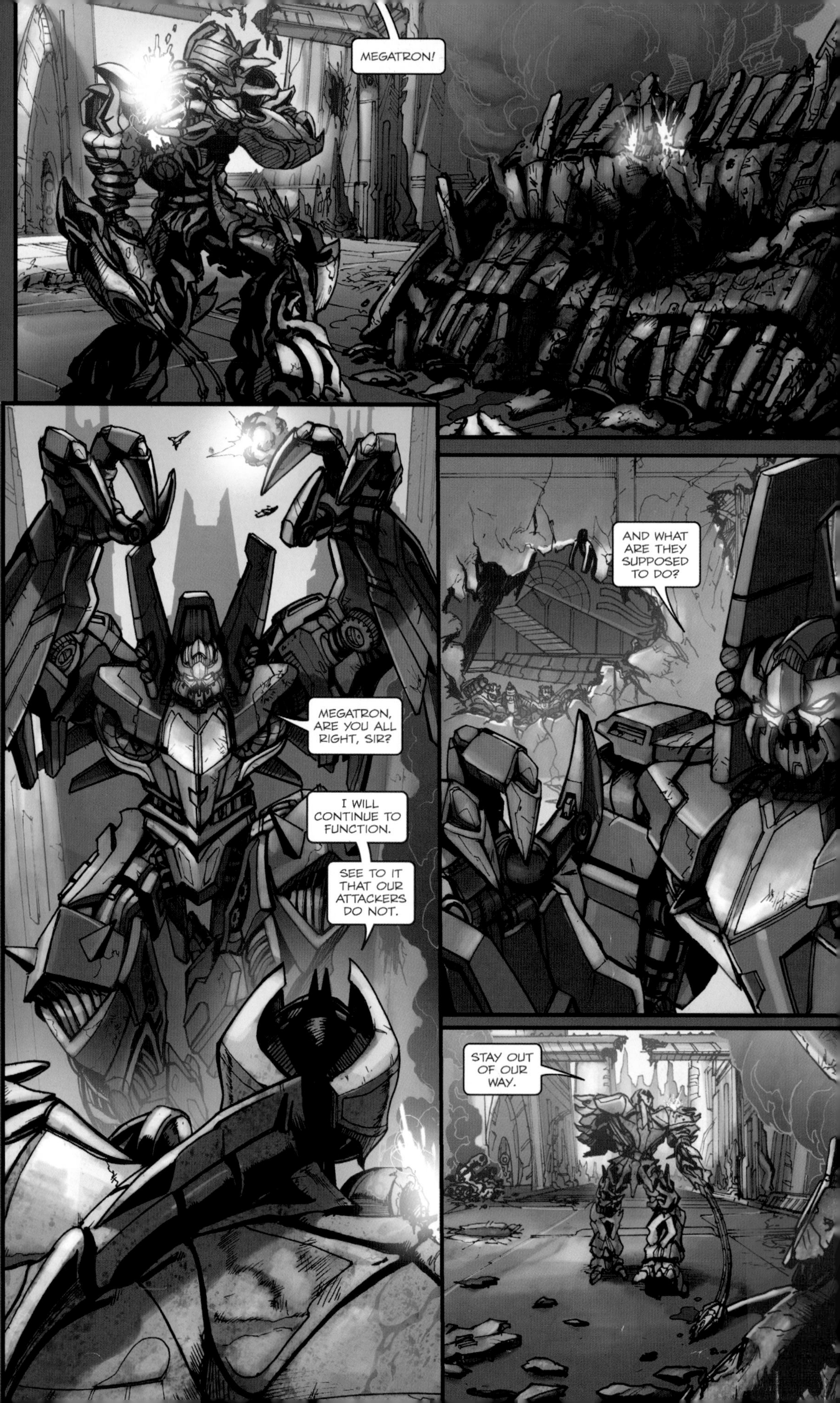
MEGATRON!
MEGATRON, ARE YOU ALL RIGHT, SIR?
I WILL CONTINUE TO FUNCTION.
SEE TO IT THAT OUR ATTACKERS DO NOT.
AND WHAT ARE THEY SUPPOSED TO DO?
STAY OUT OF OUR WAY.

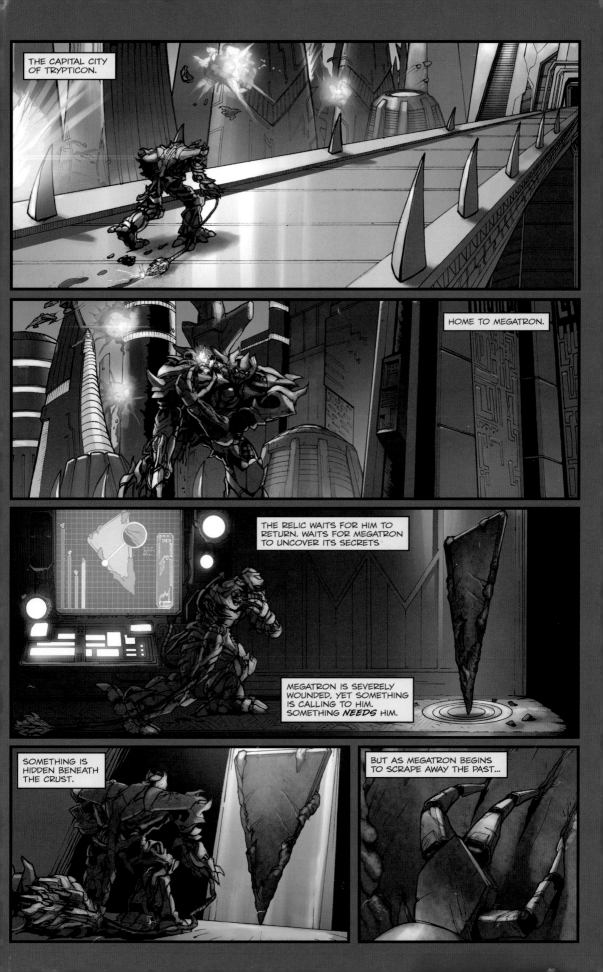

THE CAPITAL CITY OF TRYPTICON.

HOME TO MEGATRON.

THE RELIC WAITS FOR HIM TO RETURN. WAITS FOR MEGATRON TO UNCOVER ITS SECRETS.

MEGATRON IS SEVERELY WOUNDED, YET SOMETHING IS CALLING TO HIM. SOMETHING *NEEDS* HIM.

SOMETHING IS HIDDEN BENEATH THE CRUST.

BUT AS MEGATRON BEGINS TO SCRAPE AWAY THE PAST...

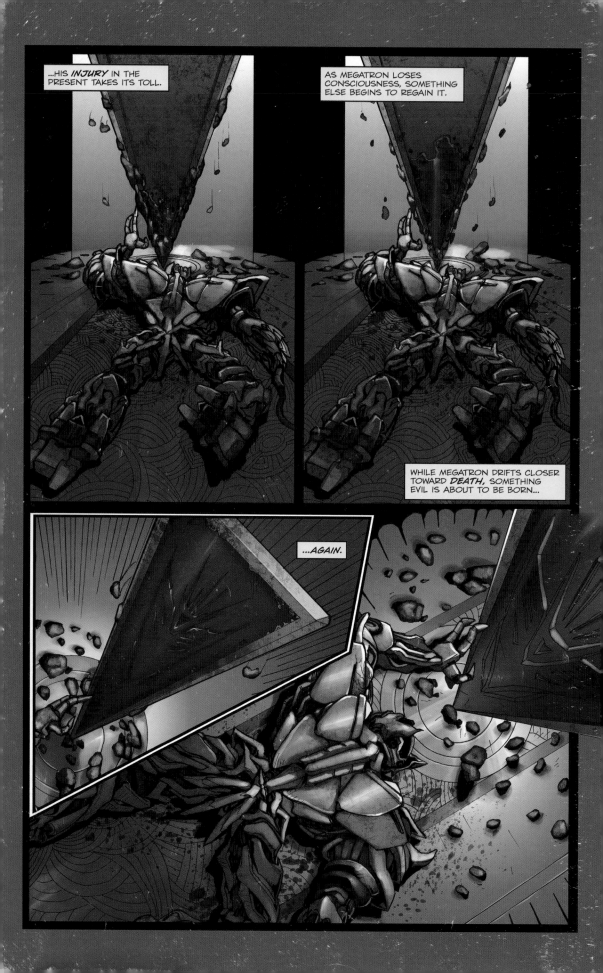

...HIS *INJURY* IN THE PRESENT TAKES ITS TOLL.

AS MEGATRON LOSES CONSCIOUSNESS, SOMETHING ELSE BEGINS TO REGAIN IT.

WHILE MEGATRON DRIFTS CLOSER TOWARD *DEATH*, SOMETHING EVIL IS ABOUT TO BE BORN...

...AGAIN.